Mark Twain's
Adventures of Tom Sawyer

Tom Sawyer
and Buried Treasure

Adapted by I.M. Richardson
Illustrated by Bert Dodson

Troll Associates

Library of Congress Cataloging in Publication Data

Richardson, I. M.
    Tom Sawyer and buried treasure.

    (Adventures of Tom Sawyer; 3)
    Summary: Tom and Huck's search for buried treasure is
interrupted by the villainous Injun Joe and his accomplice.
    [1. Missouri—Fiction. 2. Buried treasure—Fiction]
I. Dodson, Bert, ill.   II. Twain, Mark, 1835-1910.
Adventures of Tom Sawyer.   III. Title.   IV. Series:
Richardson, I. M. Adventures of Tom Sawyer.
PZ7.R3948Tob 1984   [Fic]   83-18049
ISBN 0-8167-0063-X (lib. bdg.)
ISBN 0-8167-0064-8 (pbk.)

"It's creepy out here," whispered Huckleberry Finn. It was after midnight, and Huck and Tom Sawyer were digging for buried treasure. "Sometimes there's a dead man buried with it—to keep guard," said Tom. "Lordy!" gasped Huck. Then Tom added, "S'pose this one was to stick his skull out and say something!" With that awful thought, they quit for the night. Next time, they would dig somewhere else—in the daylight.

They agreed to dig at the old haunted house on Cardiff Hill. But even in the daylight, it was dark and spooky inside the house. With pounding hearts, Tom and Huck tiptoed across the dirt floor. They listened for the slightest sound, ready to run in an instant. They spoke in whispers, daring each other to go up the stairs. Finally they tossed their shovels in the corner and crept up the creaking staircase.

They found nothing upstairs and were about to come down when they heard a voice. It was just outside the front door. There was no time to run, so Huck and Tom stretched out on the floor and waited. Two men entered. The boys recognized one of them as the deaf and dumb Spaniard they had seen around town recently. The other man was a ragged stranger.

The stranger mumbled something about a dangerous job. Then, to the boys' surprise, the "deaf and dumb" Spaniard began to speak! Huck and Tom instantly recognized the voice. It was the murderer, Injun Joe! "We'll do that dangerous job as soon as the time is right," he said. "Now it's your turn to stand watch while I catch some sleep."

A few minutes later, Injun Joe was snoring. Before long, the other man began to nod, and soon he was snoring, too. The boys drew a long, grateful breath. Tom whispered, "Now's our chance." Slowly and softly he stood up and took a step. The old floor gave a loud creak, and Tom sank back down, almost dead with fright.

When the men awoke, they raised a loose hearthstone and pulled out a bag that had been hidden underneath. They each took some silver coins from the bag. "Let's bury the rest much deeper this time," said Injun Joe. He knelt down and began digging with his bowie knife. Suddenly the metal blade struck something hard. "What's this?" he said. "Half-rotten plank, I think. No, it's a box."

He poked his hand through a hole in the top of the box and brought out a handful of coins. "It's gold!" he cried. "Bring me that old shovel from over in the corner." A moment later, an old wooden box was dragged out and opened. "Why, there's thousands here!" exclaimed Injun Joe. Upstairs, the boys trembled with excitement. Injun Joe's partner said, "Now you don't need to do that other job."

"This doesn't change a thing," growled Injun Joe. "That other job is for *revenge!*" His partner grunted, "Well, all right. But what should we do with the gold—bury it again?" Injun Joe replied, "Yes—no! There was fresh dirt on that shovel. That means somebody was here—and not too long ago. I'll take it to my den—Number Two, under the cross. The box will be safe there."

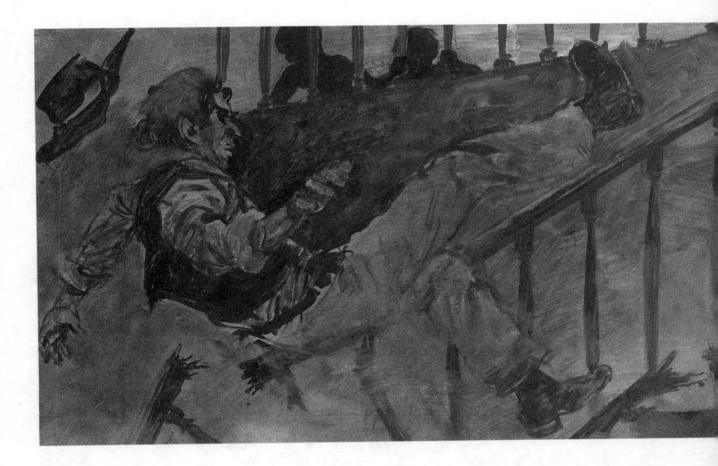

Then he added, "Whoever brought those shovels might still be here. Maybe they're upstairs—hiding." Silent panic swept across the boys' faces. They listened in terror as heavy footsteps climbed the creaking stairs. Suddenly the rotten timbers splintered, and the staircase came crashing to the ground. Injun Joe struggled to his feet, grumbling. A few minutes later, the two men carried off the box of gold.

Tom and Huck climbed down, feeling sorry for themselves. "We should've hidden the shovels. Then Injun Joe would've buried the gold again," groaned Huck. "And while he was off getting his revenge," added Tom, "we could have dug it up!" They decided to keep an eye out for Injun Joe. If they saw him, they would follow him to "Number Two"—wherever that might be.

The next day, Tom could think of nothing but the treasure. "Listen, Huck," he said. "Maybe Number Two is Room Number Two in the Temperance Inn." The back door of Room Number Two opened out onto an alley. All week long the boys watched it, but they didn't see Injun Joe enter or leave. Tom decided to try for a closer look. Maybe he could even get inside and search for the treasure!

One dark night, Tom met Huck outside the alley. He held
his aunt's tin lantern, wrapped in a towel to block the light.
As Huck stood guard out in the street, Tom sneaked into
the alley. He crept up to the back door of Room Number
Two and silently reached for the doorknob. His heart was
beating so fast he could hardly catch his breath.

Suddenly Tom came tearing out past Huck, crying, "Run! Run for your life!" The two boys didn't stop until they reached the other end of the village. When Tom caught his breath, he said, "Huck, it was awful! I tried the door, and it wasn't locked! I went in and shined the light and *great Caesar's ghost!*" Huck's eyes were wide as saucers. "What'd you see?" he gasped.

"Huck, I almost stepped on Injun Joe's hand!" cried Tom.
"He was layin' there on the floor—passed out, I guess. His
arms were spread out, and he didn't budge. I grabbed the
lantern and ran. Huck, let's not try anything else till we
know he's not in there. It's too scary." Huck agreed. "I'll
watch the place every night," he said. "When Injun Joe
leaves, I'll get you, and we'll search his den for the
treasure."

16

On Saturday, Tom put thoughts of Injun Joe and the treasure aside. Becky Thatcher was having a picnic down near McDougal's Cave. All her schoolmates were going. The old steam ferry had been chartered for the day, and the happy group climbed aboard. By mid-morning, they were headed down the river.

As soon as the ferry had tied up, the crowd went ashore. The woods and hills near McDougal's Cave began to echo with shouts and laughter. Several hours later, everyone wandered back, tired and hungry. Soon the picnic baskets were brought out, and the feast began. Afterward, someone shouted, "Who's ready for the cave?" Everyone was.

McDougal's Cave was a vast maze of crooked tunnels that led nowhere. You could wander for days and never find the end of the huge limestone caverns. No one knew the cave completely, but everyone knew the passages that were near the entrance. So small groups of boys and girls could secretly slip off and disappear, only to spring out somewhere else, surprising the rest of the party.

By and by, one group after another came straggling back to the mouth of the cave with dripping candles and dirty clothes. The sun had already set. Everyone had forgotten all about the time, and the ferry's clanging bell had been calling them for half an hour. At last, the ferry was pushing up the river toward home, filled with weary passengers.

20

Huck Finn saw the lights of the returning ferry, but he didn't pay much attention. He was too busy watching and waiting for Injun Joe to come out of Room Number Two. By eleven o'clock, the lights at the inn were put out, and darkness was everywhere. Huck began to wonder if he should give up and go to sleep in Ben Rogers's hayloft. After all, maybe this wasn't even where the treasure was hidden.

Suddenly the door to Room Number Two opened. Huck disappeared into the shadows near the corner. The next moment, two men came out of the alley, and one of them was carrying a bundle under his arm. "The treasure!" thought Huck. *Should he go get Tom? No,* he thought, *there was not enough time.* So he followed the men by himself. He had to find out where they were taking the treasure.

As Huck glided along behind them, his bare feet made no sound at all. He kept far behind them as they moved through the village. Then they started up the path that led up Cardiff Hill. He followed them past the Welshman's house, past the old quarry, and right to the top of the hill. Finally they disappeared into a narrow path between some bushes.

Huck crept closer. It was too dark to see a thing. Suddenly a man cleared his throat not four feet away! Huck's heart shot into his throat, and he stood there shaking. They were just outside the Widow Douglas's yard. "Her lights are still on. She must have company," muttered Injun Joe. "This is too dangerous," said the other man. He was the ragged stranger from the haunted house.

"We'll wait till the lights go out," said Injun Joe. "Then I'll get my revenge. The widow's husband was the justice of the peace who threw me in jail. And that ain't all. He had me *horsewhipped!* Right in front of the jail, with the whole town looking on. Then he went and died, before I could get even. But tonight, I'll take out my revenge on his widow."

Huck tiptoed back—carefully, slowly, one silent step at a time. SNAP! A twig broke under his foot. His breath stopped, and he listened. Apparently the men had not heard it. So Huck turned around without making another sound and slipped down the path. When he reached the quarry, he felt safe, and he began to run. A few minutes later he was banging on the Welshman's door.

Three minutes later, the old Welshman and his two sturdy sons were running up the path with guns in their hands. Huck hid behind a huge boulder and listened. There was a long, anxious silence. Suddenly the stillness was shattered by the sound of gunfire, and someone cried out. Huck didn't wait to find out what had happened. He fled down the hill and into the night.

At dawn, Huck learned that the two men had escaped. He gave a description of the deaf and dumb Spaniard and the ragged stranger to the Welshman's sons, who rushed off to tell the sheriff. Suddenly the Welshman said, "Huck! You said you overheard the two men *talking*. If the Spaniard is deaf and dumb, he can't speak!" Huck leaned closer and whispered, "He ain't a Spaniard—he's Injun Joe!"

Then Huck begged, "Oh, please don't say I told you!" The Welshman promised not to mention Huck's name. Then the old man said, "Last night, my sons and I took a good look around up there. And we found a bundle of—" "OF WHAT?" cried Huck. The words shot out before he could stop them. The color drained from his face. His eyes were wide and anxious. He held his breath. "Why, burglar tools," said the Welshman.

Huck let his breath out slowly in relief. The old man said, "Now, what did *you* think we'd found?" Huck didn't want to say. He didn't want anyone to know about the treasure until he and Tom had it safely in their own hands. What answer could he give the Welshman? Without thinking, he said, "Sunday-school books, maybe?" The old man threw back his head and roared with laughter.

Huck turned the facts over in his mind. The treasure was still a secret. Since Injun Joe's bundle had contained only burglar tools, the treasure must still be in Number Two. No one but Tom and Huck knew that. So everything was going to turn out all right, after all! Right now, all he and Tom had to do was wait.

Meanwhile, the sheriff had formed a posse, which was out searching the countryside. Without a doubt, Injun Joe and his partner would be captured and thrown in jail before nightfall. Then Tom and Huck could go to the Temperance Inn and search Number Two without fear of being discovered. And then the treasure would finally be theirs!